There Were Monkeys in my Kitchen!

Sheree Fitch   Marc Mongeau

DOUBLEDAY

TORONTO NEW YORK LONDON SYDNEY AUCKLAND

To my brother Shawn and sister Leanne
with memories of dancing days
in Monkey-town, New Brunswick
S.F.

To Matilde, my daughter
M.M.

Copyright © 1992 by Sheree Fitch (text)
Copyright © 1992 by Marc Mongeau (illustrations)
Paperback edition 1994
Reprinted 1995, 1996

The author gratefully acknowledges the assistance of the Canada Council Arts Grants in 1989.

Design by Tania Craan
Printed and bound in Canada

Canadian Cataloguing in Publication Data
Fitch, Sheree
    There were monkeys in my kitchen!

ISBN 0-385-25349-4 (hardcover);0-385-25470-9 (paperback)

I. Mongeau, Marc. II. Title.

PS8561.i86t54 1992 jC813'.54 C91-095153-5
PZ7.F57th 1992

Published in Canada by Doubleday Canada Limited
105 Bond Street, Toronto, Ontario M5B 1Y3

There were monkeys in my kitchen.

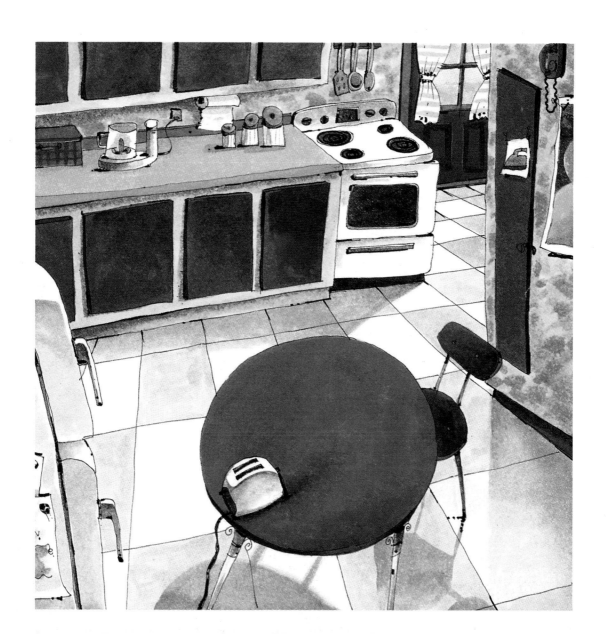

There were monkeys
In my kitchen
They were climbing
Up the walls
They were dancing
On the ceiling
They were bouncing
Basketballs

Now ...
You might think
That sounds funny
Now ...
You might think
That sounds neat
To see a thousand
Monkeys dancing
To a funky
Monkey beat

BUT ...
Let me tell you
It was terrible
Hardest day
I ever had
I was there
So believe me
It was bad
IT WAS BAD.

First there were gorillas
In a grand ballet
Pirouette
Arabesque
Plié
Sauté

They wore ballerina slippers
And purple fishnet socks
And when they danced
The city shook
For forty-nine blocks

So ...

I called the police
I called the RCMP
I was fairly polite
I even said "please"
As I shouted in the phone:

CH-CH-CH-CHIMPANZEES!

Then quicker than it takes
To do a double-duty sneeze
I turned around
And in my face
Were forty MORE…
Chimpanzees!

They wag-wiggled
They jag-jiggled
One said,
"If you please
You may call me by my proper name –
Deb-or-ah Louise."

She said,
"I am just a go-go ape
I go-go everywhere
In my red leather boots
With my punky monkey hair."

So ...

I called the police
I dialed nine-one-one
I said,
"I think you'd better hurry up
THIS HOUSE HAS COME UNDONE!"

The next thing I knew
Those apes were playing rock 'n' roll
They were twisting on the table
And broke my cereal bowl

They were dancing to the Beatles
(That's an old singing group)
And they crumbled up crackers
In my minestrone soup.

Then they turned up the volume
On my brother's ghetto blaster
They got clumsy
They got goofy
They danced
Faster
Faster
FASTER

So I shouted in the phone:
"It's a
NATIONAL
IRRATIONAL
PRIMORDIAL
DISASTER!"

But ...

Before I had the time
To give the number
Of our street
I was interrupted rudely
By a crash–bang beat

There were fifty-five monkeys
Singing   Do-si-do!
Saying   YEE-HAW!
            GET DOWN!
            SWING YER PARTNER
            BY THE TOE!

PROMENADE!
LEMONADE!
DO-SI-DO!

They swirled and twirled
In crinolined skirts
They wore ten gallon hats
They had rhinestones
In their shirts

So ...

I called the police
I said,
"What can you do?
Has anyone reported
Monkeys missing from the zoo?"

Then ...

Coming from the basement
Was a slow soft song
I peeked and saw
Orangutans
Tangoing along

They were dipping
They were slipping
They were flipping
Right out

So I got irritated and
I heard myself shout,
"You apes have got to get!
All monkeys have to go!"
Then they all stopped dancing
And they shouted at me,
"NO!"

So ...

I called the police
And a security guard
I said,
"Come get these apes!
Get them out of my yard!"

For I'd already seen
All those monkeys on the lawn
They were playing croquet
They had gold shoes on

Some were dancing on the clothesline
Some were swinging from the trees
Hilarious
Gregarious
Chimpanzees

Then …

Coming from upstairs
Was a wheezy whining sound
So I ran right up
I took a peek
I took a look around

There were monkeys
In my bedroom
They were messing up
My quilts
One was playing
Bagpipes
They were wearing
Tartan kilts

One said,
"You can call me MacIntosh."
He did the highland fling
One said,
"Kookachica burra."
But I didn't say a thing

I just ...

Called the police
And the FBI
And Scotland Yard
And a private eye

I said, "This place is CHAOS!"
I said, "BABOON catastrophe!
You folks have got to help!
You've got to rescue me!"

Because ...

Those apes had taken bubblebath
And dumped it in the tub
They played Hawaiian music
They did the hula as they scrubbed

Well …
I watched for a minute
Then I went and jumped right in it
(Don't know why …
Just thought I'd try)
But as soon as I got dry …

I called the police
I called the RCMP
I was *extra* polite
I said "Pretty, pretty *please*"
As I shouted out,
"HELP!"
Ch-Ch-Ch-Chimpanzees!

Some gorillas crunched granola
Some were eating toast and peas
Some were slurping macaroni
Topped with gorgonzola cheese

So I got down on my knees

I said, "This place is chaos!"
I cried, "A complete CATASTROPHE!"
I sobbed, "I want my mama!"
I sniffed, "Woe begone is me …"

So …

I went to the kitchen sink
Which is a place where I think and think (and think)
Then suddenly I had an idea
The solution to save the day
I shouted out one word:
"BANANAS!!!"
And all those monkeys stopped.

I said, "Now that I have your attention,
 I'd like all you monkeys, chimpanzees, apes and gorillas
TO GO! GET! SCADADDLE!
HURRY UP! GET OUT OF THIS PLACE!

Well ....

One monkey came right over
One wiped my tears away
She said, "I guess that we should go
That's all you had to say ..."

Then one said,
"My name is Aristotle."
One said,
"Call me Socrates."

I said,
"I'm really pleased to meet you
Glad to know you chimpanzees."

But ...

Just then I heard a siren
And I knew my help had come
There were forty-nine Mounties
They were blowing bubblegum

I said,
"This is no time for chewing
This is no time for bubbles
I tell you that this neighborhood
Has got its share of troubles."

"I'm Inspector Lea-Ann Jane."
Said a woman dressed in red
"Can you tell us what your name is?"
"Well, uh, Willa Wellowby," I said.

"Well, Welluh Willa Wellowby
You have called us
Several times
Said you had some monkey business?
Now we're here to solve these crimes ..."

Then she blew the biggest bubble
So I burst it in her face
"Look," I said, "Chimpanzees!"
All over this place!"

And she said,
"Where???"

Now you probably won't believe me
But those monkeys were all gone
No monkeys in the kitchen
No monkeys on the lawn
No monkeys on the clothesline
They had left the neighborhood

There, I thought
It's over,
I guess those apes have gone
For good

The Inspector was not smiling
She said,
"Is this a false alarm???
Should I send you to the zoo
Or, perhaps, a monkey farm???"

I said …

"But there WERE monkeys
In my kitchen
They were climbing
Up the walls
They WERE dancing
On the ceiling
They were bouncing
Basketballs …"

"Indeed," said the Inspector.
"We do not have the time
We Mounties are too busy
We're off to solve another crime."

So …
Everything was over
No dancing apes around
I found the house a little quiet
I sort of missed the monkey sound …

But …

I think I saw an elephant
Just open up my door
And I've got this funny feeling
There are
  several
    hundred
      more